DINOSAURS
Nature Activity Book

James Kavanagh
Illustrations By Raymond Leung
Junior Editor: Camille Maarse

Text & illustrations © 2011, 2021 Waterford Press Inc. All rights reserved.
No part of this work may be reproduced in any form by any graphic or electronic means, including information storage and retrieval systems without the prior written permission of the publisher.
Printed in the USA. For permissions or further information, contact Waterford Press, 1040 Harbor Lake Drive, Safety Harbor (Tampa), FL 34695.
To order, call 800-434-2555; Fax: 727-330-7765
To share comments, email us at editor@waterfordpress.com
For information on custom-published products, call 800-434-2555.
ISBN: 978-1-58355-578-1

Word Search

Say it, then find it.

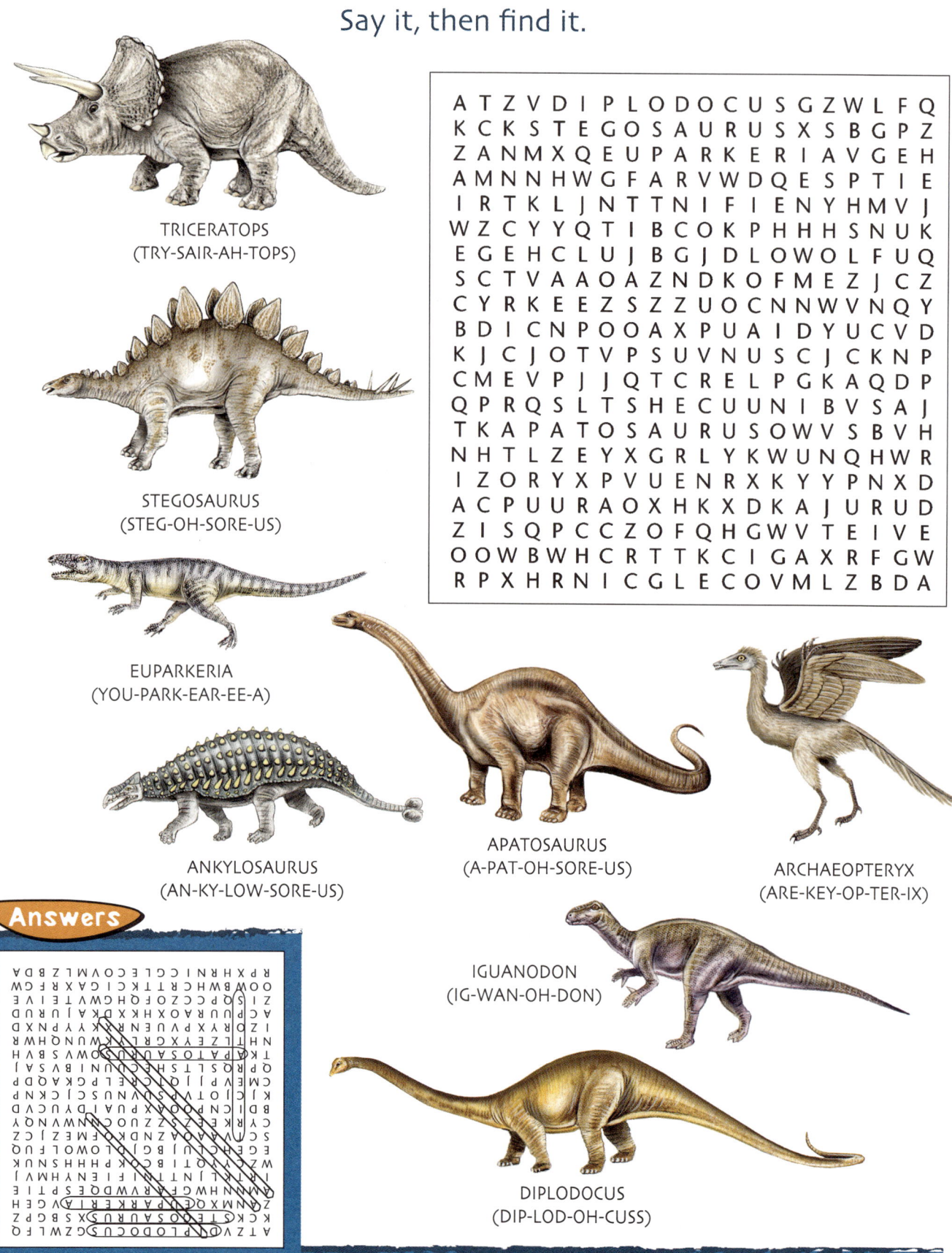

```
A T Z V D I P L O D O C U S G Z W L F Q
K C K S T E G O S A U R U S X S B G P Z
Z A N M X Q E U P A R K E R I A V G E H
A M N N H W G F A R V W D Q E S P T I E
I R T K L J N T T N I F I E N Y H M V J
W Z C Y Y Q T I B C O K P H H H S N U K
E G E H C L U J B G J D L O W O L F U Q
S C T V A A O A Z N D K O F M E Z J C Z
C Y R K E E Z S Z Z U O C N N W V N Q Y
B D I C N P O O A X P U A I D Y U C V D
K J C J O T V P S U V N U S C J C K N P
C M E V P J J Q T C R E L P G K A Q D P
Q P R Q S L T S H E C U U N I B V S A J
T K A P A T O S A U R U S O W V S B V H
N H T L Z E Y X G R L Y K W U N Q H W R
I Z O R Y X P V U E N R X K Y Y P N X D
A C P U U R A O X H K X D K A J U R U D
Z I S Q P C C Z O F Q H G W V T E I V E
O O W B W H C R T T K C I G A X R F G W
R P X H R N I C G L E C O V M L Z B D A
```

TRICERATOPS (TRY-SAIR-AH-TOPS)

STEGOSAURUS (STEG-OH-SORE-US)

EUPARKERIA (YOU-PARK-EAR-EE-A)

ANKYLOSAURUS (AN-KY-LOW-SORE-US)

APATOSAURUS (A-PAT-OH-SORE-US)

ARCHAEOPTERYX (ARE-KEY-OP-TER-IX)

IGUANODON (IG-WAN-OH-DON)

DIPLODOCUS (DIP-LOD-OH-CUSS)

Answers

A-Mazing!

The **Protoceratops** had a large bony neck frill and a parrot-like beak. Nesting sites of this species containing clutches of unhatched eggs have been found in the Gobi Desert in Mongolia.

Help this dino find its eggs.

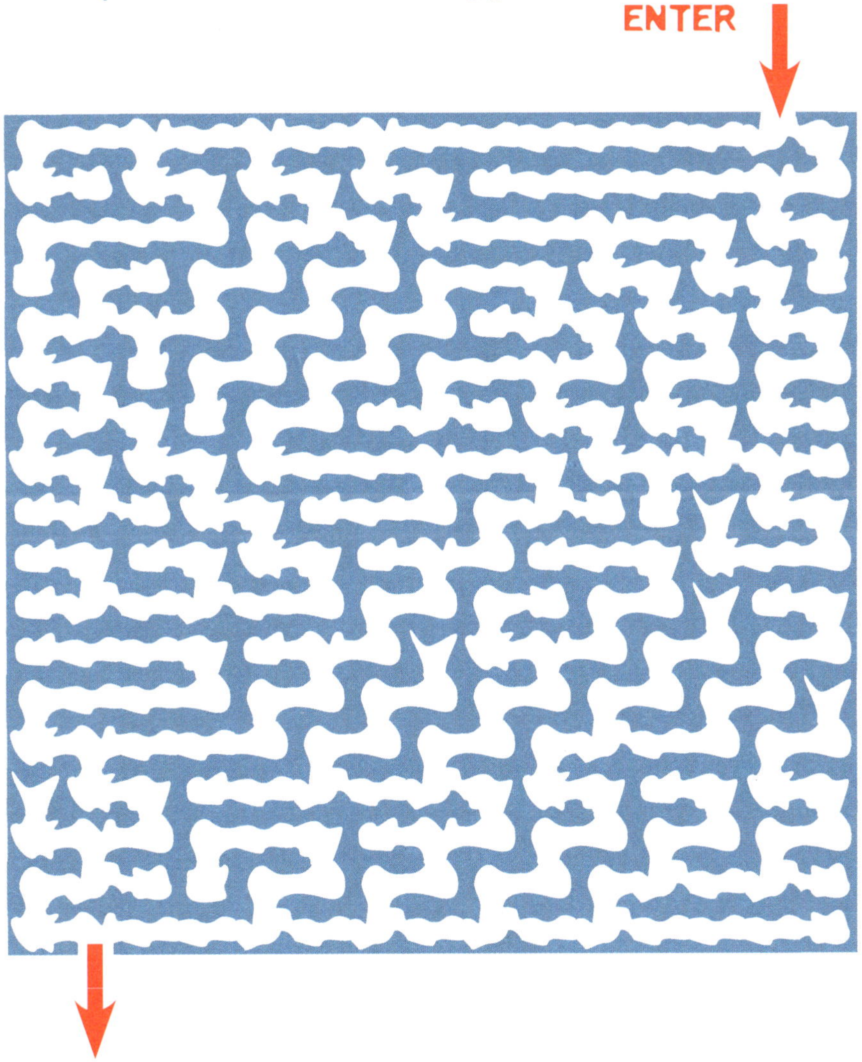

Carnivore or Herbivore

Carnivores (C) eat meat, herbivores (H) eat plants.
Circle the correct letter to note what each dinosaur eats.

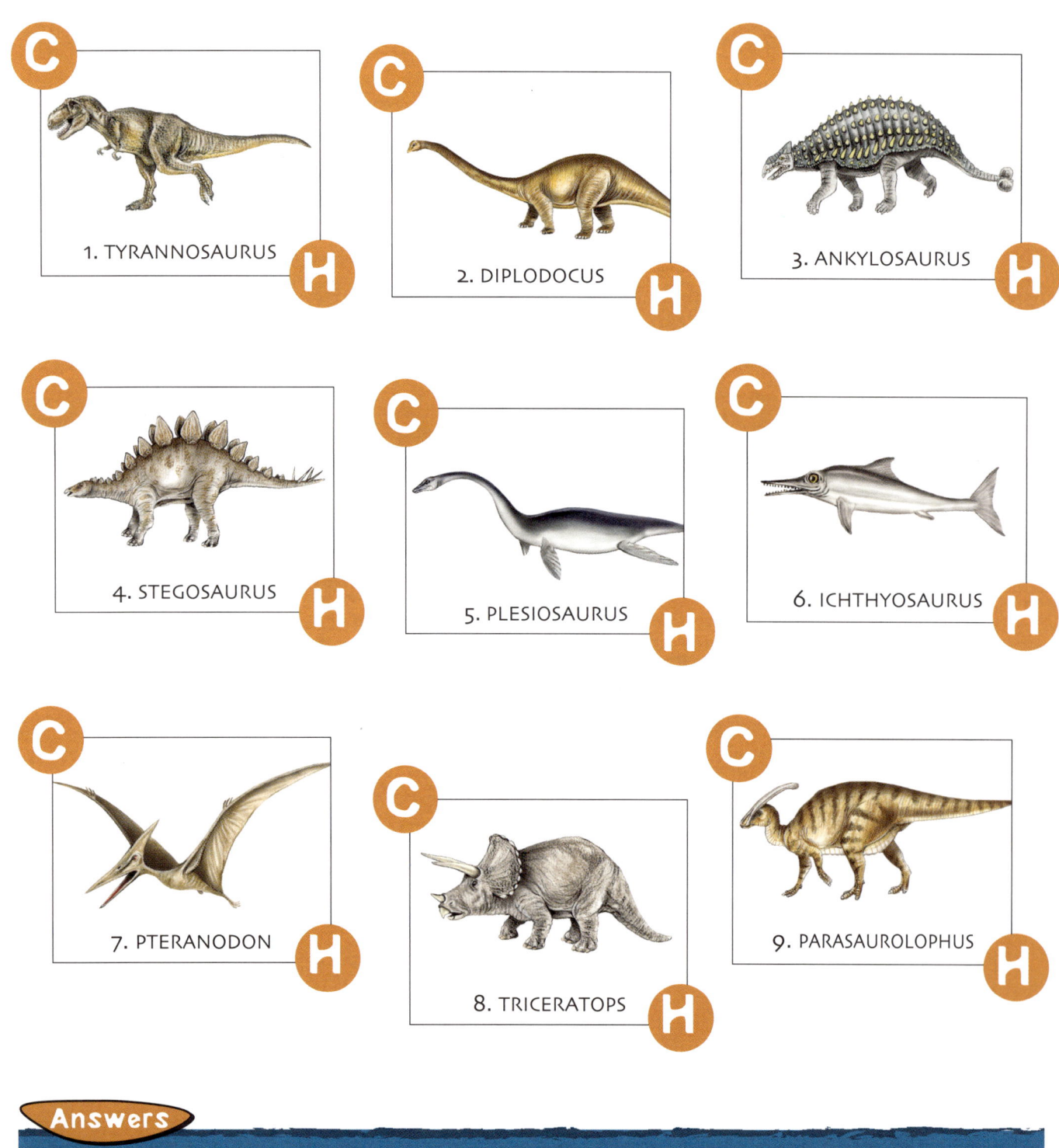

Answers

1. C 2. H 3. H 4. H 5. C 6. C 7. C 8. H 9. H

Origami

Starting with a square piece of paper, follow the simple folding instructions below to create a Plesiosaurus.

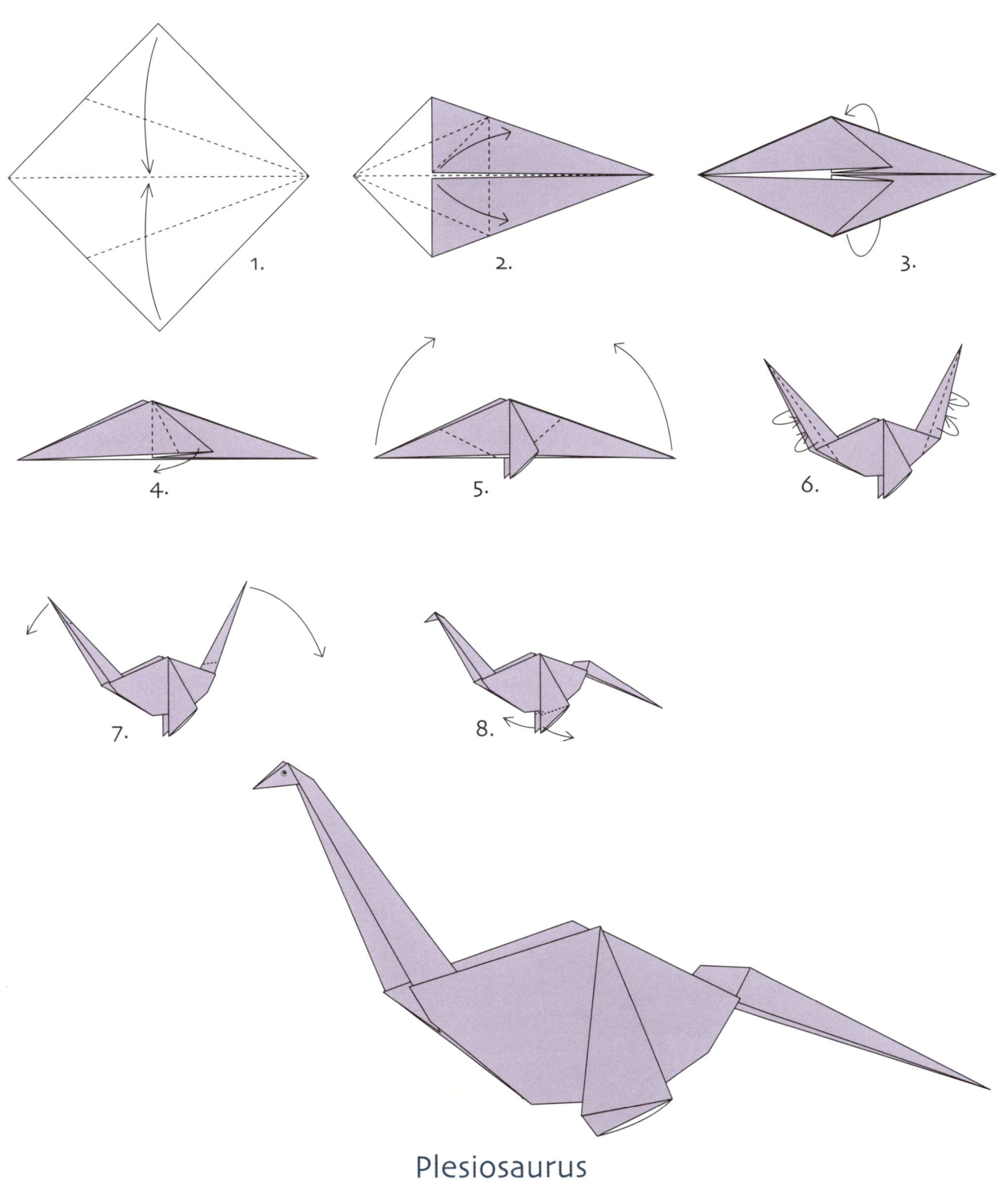

Plesiosaurus

Color Me

Dimetrodon

color key

Psittacosaurus

color key

Name Match

Draw a line between the dinosaur and its name.

1. [Chasmosaurus image]
2. [Pachycephalosaurus image]
3. [Deinonychus image]
4. [Pteranodon image]

- DEINONYCHUS
- STEGOSAURUS
- CHASMOSAURUS
- TYRANNOSAURUS
- PTERANODON
- IGUANODON
- ANKYLOSAURUS
- PACHY-CEPHALOSAURUS

5. [Stegosaurus image]
6. [Iguanodon image]
7. [Tyrannosaurus image]
8. [Ankylosaurus image]

Answers: 1. Chasmosaurus 2. Pachycephalosaurus 3. Deinonychus 4. Pteranodon 5. Stegosaurus 6. Iguanodon 7. Tyrannosaurus 8. Ankylosaurus

Spot the Differences

Spot 10 differences between the two images.

Answers

Word Search

Say it, then find it.

```
E D M X S G L I Q P K H K K V L P T L U
G D W H Q D K Z U Q K Z Y R K X P O E D
Q B S A U R C R L Y H P I L P M B V M O
Y M G I V G W W F K P I O T O L A B N S
M Z V P J I M A H E M D P Y U N C H G X
X N T T S V J B Z M C I G R Z P O K P C
O V M E P I S M Q O O C V A Z S E M D Z
N M I R P X T V O T Z H P N A L L T U Q
C F N A E K N T B W N T Z N Q Q O O L S
Q R W N F L C K A J I H F O E Y P O I R
D J D O R Z P I R C M Y O S X Z H P G O
L R T D L E Y N Y J O O G A H W Y W S O
M C N O W I K V O U S S C U N Y S M N W
F T N N O A D M N N A A A R Y U I B C A
Y N H G E R F S Y X S U M U K T S Q E Q
U P A J A H E Q X F A R E S R K P C E F
G Z W I U W P S M J U U Q H T U V O B Z
D E W V T E S U P E R S A U R U S E C N
E L A S M O S A U R U S D T O P D Q J K
N L I E D M O N T O S A U R U S Y E R Q
```

EDMONTOSAURUS
(ED-MONT-OH-SORE-US)

HYLONOMUS
(HY-LOW-NOME-US)

ELASMOSAURUS
(EH-LAZ-MOE-SORE-US)

MOSASAURUS
(MOE-SA-SORE-US)

SUPERSAURUS
(SOUP-ER-SORE-US)

BARYONYX
(BEAR-EE-ON-IX)

ICHTHYOSAURUS
(IK-THEE-OH-SORE-US)

Answers

9

Picture Scramble

Arrange the numbers in the lettered boxes to create the image on the left.

ARCHELON

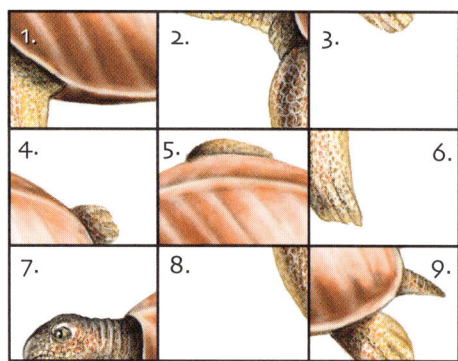

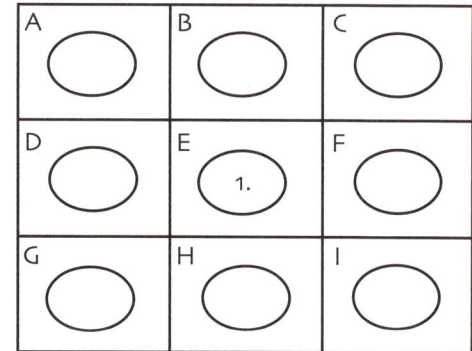

PROTOCERATOPS

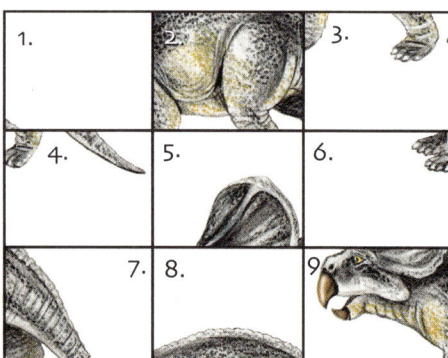

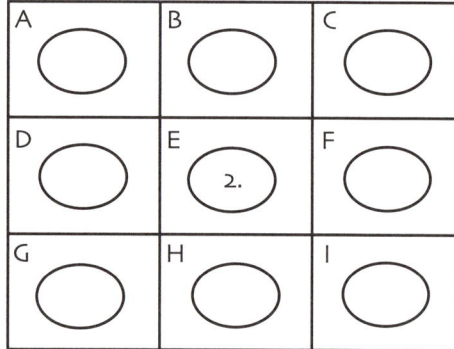

MEGATHERIUM

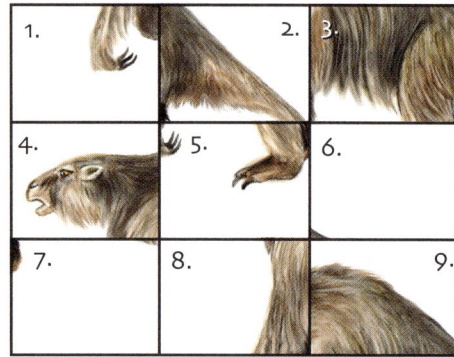

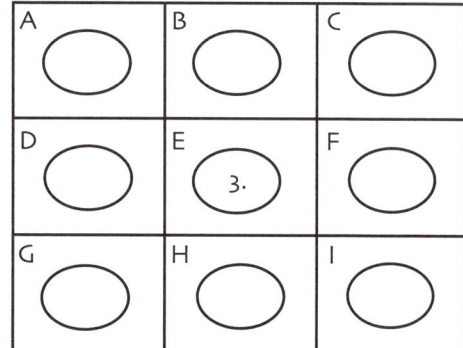

Answers

Archelon – A7, B5, C4, D2, E1, F9, G8, H6, I3

Protoceratops – A5, B8, C1, D9, E2, F7, G6, H3, I4

Megatherium – A4, B9, C6, D8, E3, F2, G1, H5, I7

Make Words

Coelacanth

Thought to be extinct for over 70 million years, this fish with limb-like fins was rediscovered off the coast of South Africa in 1938. Several more have been caught since then.

How many words can you make from the letters in its name?

Answers

Possible answers include: No, to, ho, he, el, toe, hoe, can, ant, hat, hot, lot, cat, cot, con, not, ale, ace, coal, hole, hate, late, lace, clot, cone, coat, talc, cane, neat, oleo, talc, noel, note, heat, clan, tone, hole, hone, lone, cone, cane, lane, hale, heal, teal, hotel, clean

Crossword

Across

1. Three-horned dinosaur.

3. Had bony club at the end of its tail.

5. Flying dinosaur.

2. Dinosaur with large plates down its back.

4. Super-sized dinosaur.

6. Large marine dinosaur.

Down

1. _____ Rex.

7. Long-fanged cat.

Answers

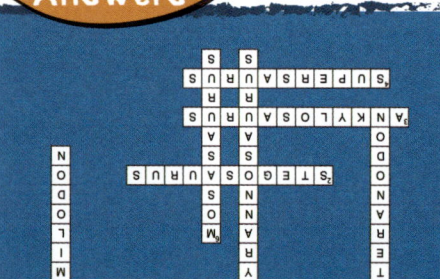

A-Mazing!

The Tyrannosaurus was a fearsome predator at the top of the Cretaceous food chain. It had teeth up to 12 in. (30 cm) long, it was up to 13 ft. (4 m) tall and weighed up to 15,000 lbs. (6818 kg)!

Help the Ornithomimus escape from the Tyrannosaurus.

ENTER

So You're Saying...

Dinosaur names are composed primarily of Latin and Greek words. For example, dino = terrible; saurus = lizard.

Draw a line between the dinosaur and the meaning of their name.

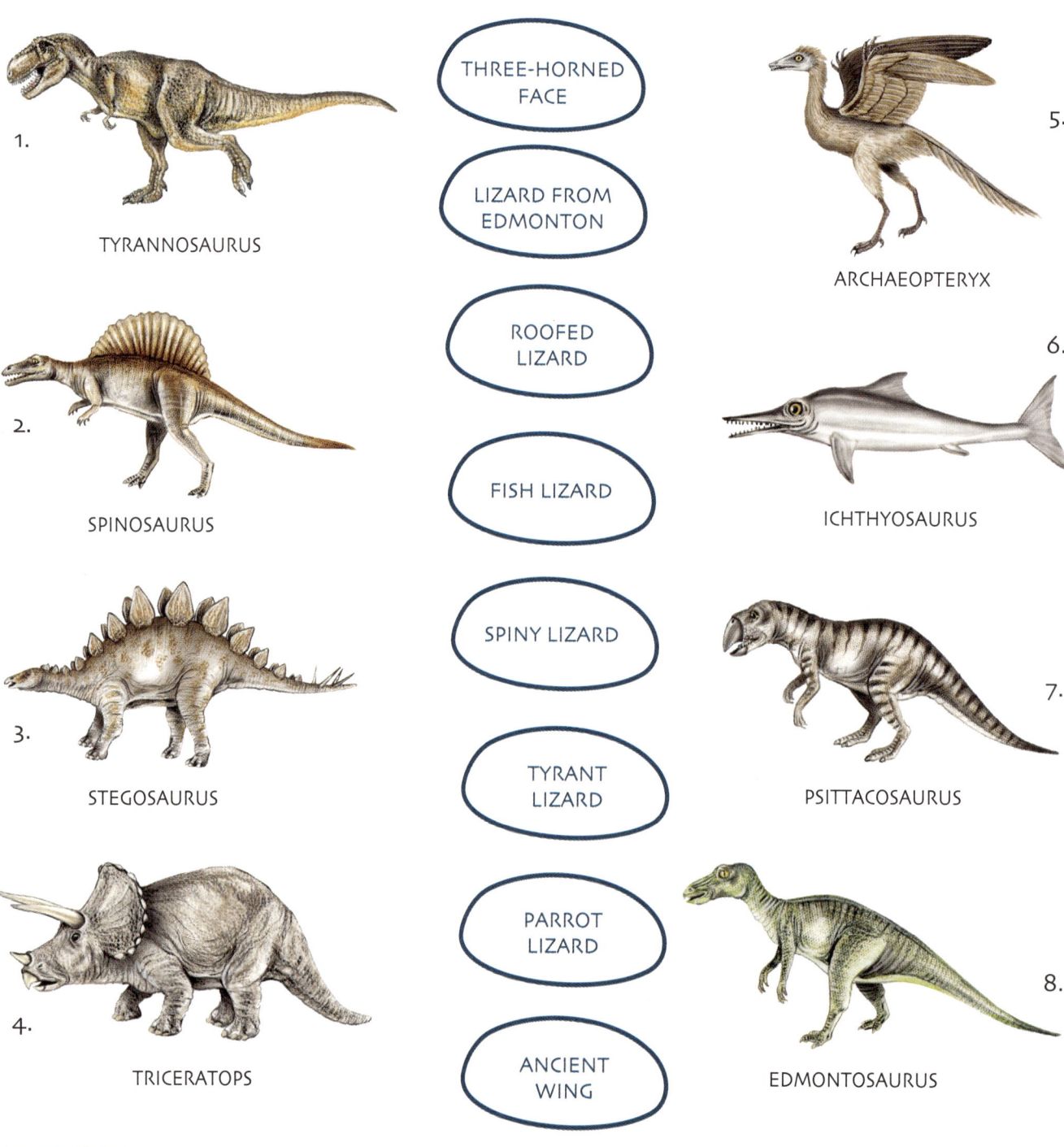

Answers

1. Tyrant lizard 2. Spiny lizard 3. Thick-headed lizard 4. Three-horned face 5. Ancient wing 6. Fish lizard 7. Parrot lizard 8. Lizard from Edmonton

Quiz

1. The huge Stegosaurus had a brain the size of a walnut.
   ☐ True   ☐ False

2. Most dinosaurs ate meat.
   ☐ True   ☐ False

3. Some dinosaurs lived in large herds like bison.
   ☐ True   ☐ False

4. The feathered lizard thought to be the ancient ancestor of birds is:
   ☐ a. Lycaenops   ☐ b. Glyptodon   ☐ c. Archaeopteryx   ☐ d. Pteranodon

5. The word dinosaur means:
   ☐ a. Huge lizard   ☐ b. Toothy lizard   ☐ c. Terrible lizard

6. The most likely reason dinosaurs went extinct is:
   ☐ a. They got sick
   ☐ b. It rained for two years and they drowned
   ☐ c. A meteor hit the earth and a dust cloud caused the plants to die, destroying their food source
   ☐ d. Earth's orbit changed and the planet became frozen during the Ice Age

7. Why did some Hadrosaurs have a large hollow head crest?
   ☐ a. To store food   ☐ b. To communicate   ☐ c. For self-defense   ☐ d. To attract a mate

8. Which dinosaur had the biggest teeth?
   ☐ a. Allosaurus   ☐ b. Tyrannosaurus   ☐ c. Compsognathus   ☐ d. Spinosaurus

9. The largest dinosaur weighed:
   ☐ a. 50 ton   ☐ b. 75 ton   ☐ c. 100 ton   ☐ d. 150 ton

10. How much meat could a Tyrannosaurus eat in one feeding?
    ☐ a. 100 lbs.   ☐ b. 250 lbs.   ☐ c. 350 lbs.   ☐ d. 500 lbs.

Answers

1. T
2. F Most dinosaurs were plant-eaters.
3. T Scientists believe several of the plant-eating dinosaurs (duck-billed dinosaurs for example) likely lived in packs because there was safety in numbers.
4. c
5. c
6. c
7. b Scientists believe the crest was a resonating chamber that was used to amplify vocalizations.
8. b Some of its teeth are over six inches long!
9. c The dinosaur Argentinosaurus is believed to have weighed 100 ton.
10. d

Shadow Know-How

Can you identify these dinosaurs?

Answers

1. Protoceratops
2. Pteranodon
3. Triceratops
4. Stegosaurus
5. Brachiosaurus
6. Plesiosaurus
7. Ichthyosaurus

Connect-the-Dots

Connect the dots in number order to reveal an ancient fossil.

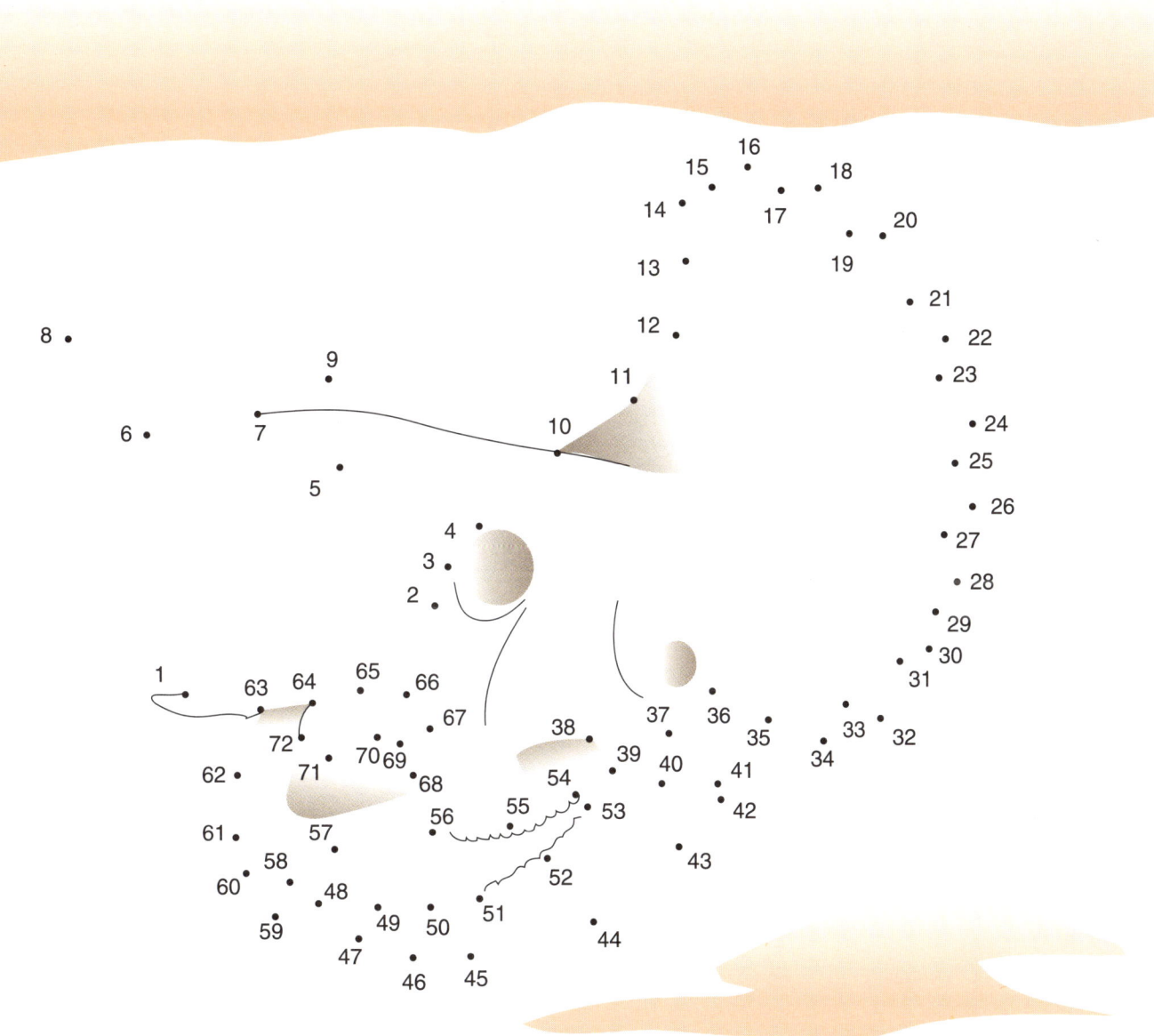

Bonus question:
What is it?

Answers

Bonus Answer: Triceratops

Name Scramble

Unscramble the letters to form the names of these ancient creatures.

1. GNTLPYOOD
2. NDOIGUAON
3. UNRASULYOKAS
4. AURUSPAATSO
5. PISUSNOUSAR
6. ONDIUECYNHS
7. NROACEHL
8. PVORITARO

Answers: 1. Glyptodon 2. Iguanodon 3. Ankylosaurus 4. Apatosaurus 5. Spinosaurus 6. Deinonychus 7. Archelon 8. Oviraptor

Picture Scramble

Arrange the numbers in the lettered boxes to create the image on the left.

ALLOSAURUS

ARCHAEOPTERYX

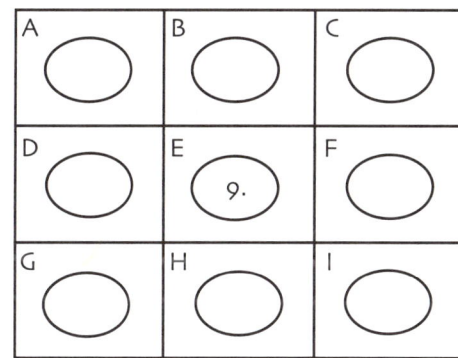

CHASMOSAURUS

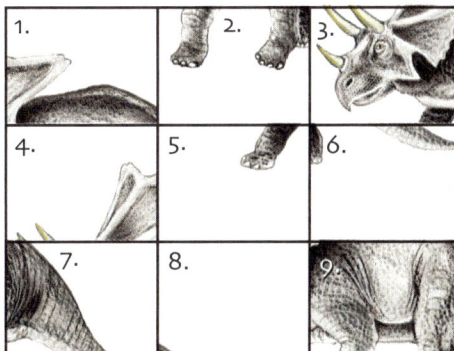

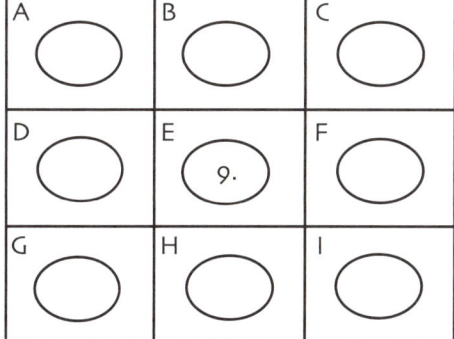

Answers

Allosaurus A5, B7, C6, D9, E4, F1, G8, H3, I2

Archaeopteryx A6, B4, C7, D1, E9, F3, G5, H2, I8

Chasmosaurus A4, B1, C8, D3, E9, F7, G5, H2, I6

19

Name Match

After the dinosaurs went extinct 65 million years ago, new and unique species began to populate the earth. Though technically not dinosaurs, many are well-represented in the fossil record. A few living species are considered "living fossils" and are almost identical to their ancient ancestors.

Draw a line between the species and its history.

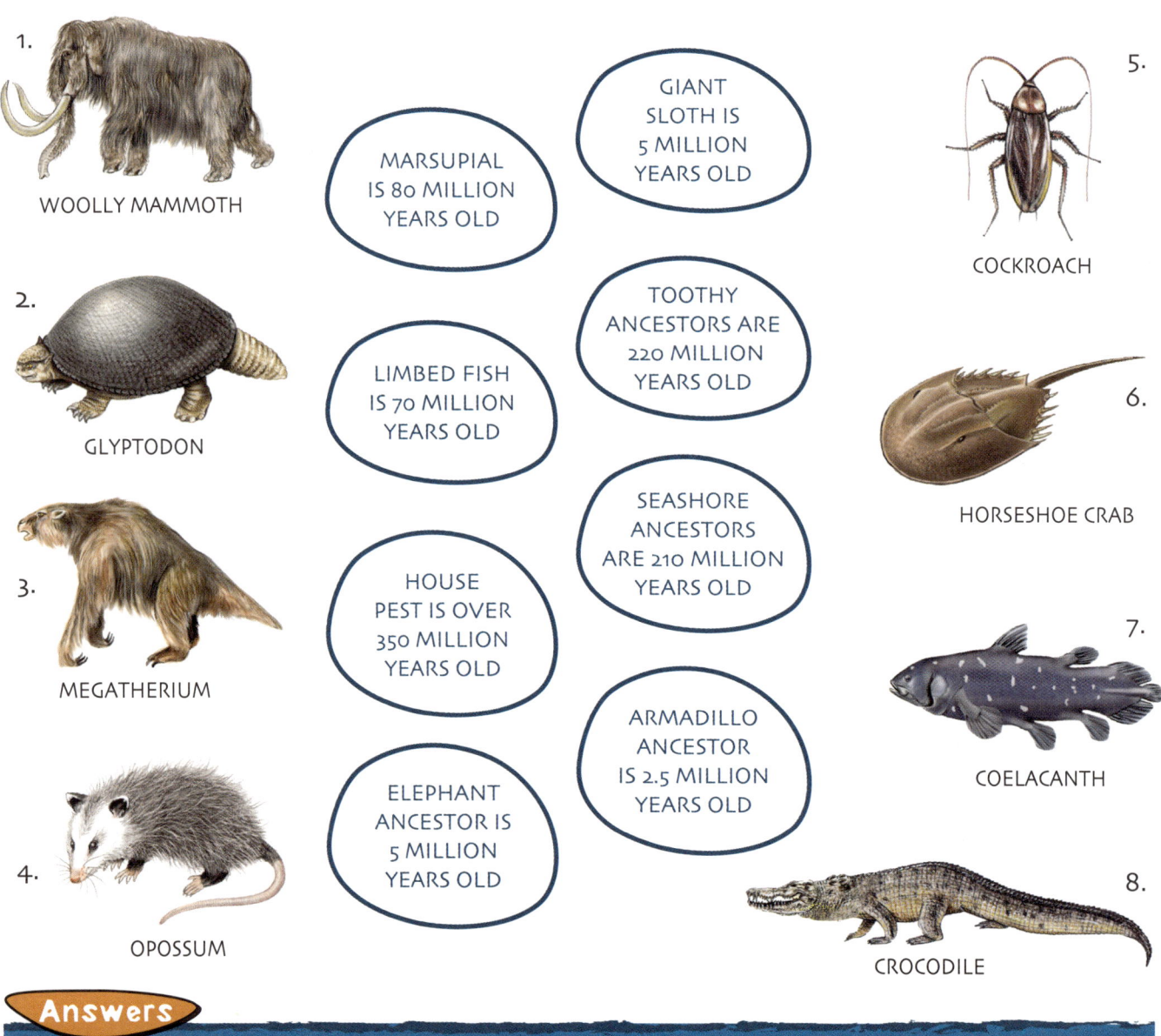

1. WOOLLY MAMMOTH
2. GLYPTODON
3. MEGATHERIUM
4. OPOSSUM
5. COCKROACH
6. HORSESHOE CRAB
7. COELACANTH
8. CROCODILE

- MARSUPIAL IS 80 MILLION YEARS OLD
- GIANT SLOTH IS 5 MILLION YEARS OLD
- TOOTHY ANCESTORS ARE 220 MILLION YEARS OLD
- LIMBED FISH IS 70 MILLION YEARS OLD
- SEASHORE ANCESTORS ARE 210 MILLION YEARS OLD
- HOUSE PEST IS OVER 350 MILLION YEARS OLD
- ARMADILLO ANCESTOR IS 2.5 MILLION YEARS OLD
- ELEPHANT ANCESTOR IS 5 MILLION YEARS OLD

Answers

1. Elephant ancestor is 5 million years old
2. Armadillo ancestor is 2.5 million years old
3. Giant sloth is 5 million years old
4. Marsupial is 80 million years old
5. House pest is over 350 million years old
6. Seashore ancestors are 210 million years old
7. Limbed fish is over 70 million years old
8. Toothy ancestors are over 220 million years old

Word Search

Say it, then find it.

```
S Z U D D Q O P L H A I P O U B A P
D D Y V O H W B F K Q L L V U J J A
G P R W N D R T G Q H E E R D B A C
C O M P S O G N A T H U S O V Z H H
L M A C R G B E Q B Q B I R H G I Y
T U A T K C G N Q R Y J O K X W X C
Z J Y I K B O Z A A E E S K E Y B E
E Q D S A L I R N C G S A N A E W P
K E Q M R S T X N H R V U E F M S H
N U A Q M U A M Q I T M R E R H O A
R F S N K C K U H O T R U A A I S L
U W R S M D Q P R S H H S V H G T O
V A G I B X G Q H A P Z O P E N K S
I N O S Z K A B P U C A F M D D F A
M G H E K R K U C R B O V M I W V U
M Y K S K M X I A U R R R U X M A R
J L L S W N F Z B S T Q T P P E U U
W M H Z W Y L I D E R Y O P S H R S
```

PLESIOSAURUS
(PLEE-ZEE-OH-SORE-US)

BRACHIOSAURUS
(BRACK-EE-OH-SORE-US)

COMPSOGNATHUS
(KOMP-SOG-NAY-THUS)

PACHYCEPHALOSAURUS
(PAK-EE-SEF-AH-LOW-SORE-US)

ORNITHOMIMUS
(OR-NITH-OH-MEEM-US)

ERYOPS
(EAR-EE-OPS)

MAIASAURA
(MY-AH-SORE-AH)

Answers

Name Match

Draw a line between the dinosaur and its name.

Answers

1. Dimetrodon
2. Elasmosaurus
3. Spinosaurus
4. Archaeopteryx
5. Baryonyx
6. Maiasaura
7. Brontosaurs
8. Parasaurolophus

Color Me

Be An Artist

Draw this Chasmosaurus by copying it one square at a time.

The **Chasmosaurus** name means "opening lizard" which refers to the large openings in its bony neck frill. The frill was merely skin stretched between bones and was not thought to be used in defense, but, more likely, to attract mates or aid it in regulating its body temperature.

A-Mazing!

Deinonychus was considered one of the most voracious dinosaur predators since it was fast, likely hunted in packs, and had an extremely large sickle-like claw on each hind foot which it used to slash its prey. Its name means "terrible-claw".

Help the Parasaurolophus escape being attacked by the pack of Deinonychus.

ENTER

Picture Scramble

Arrange the numbers in the lettered boxes to create the image on the left.

WOOLLY MAMMOTH

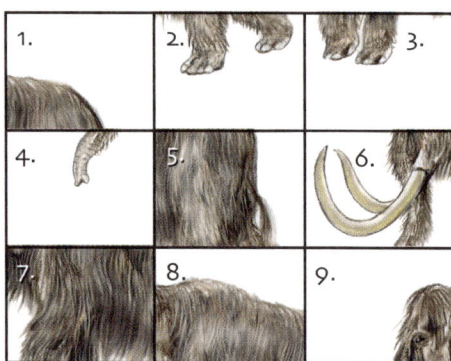

RHAMPHORHYNCHUS

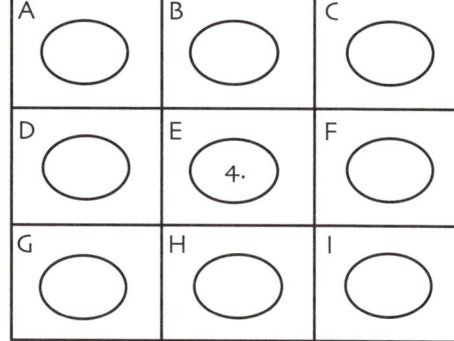

STEGOSAURUS

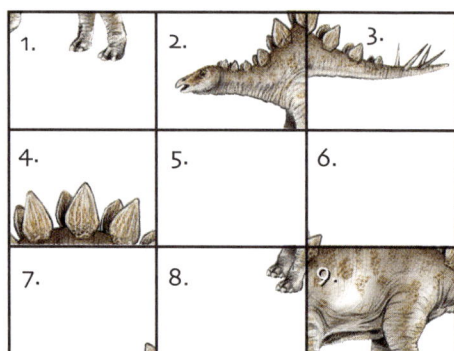

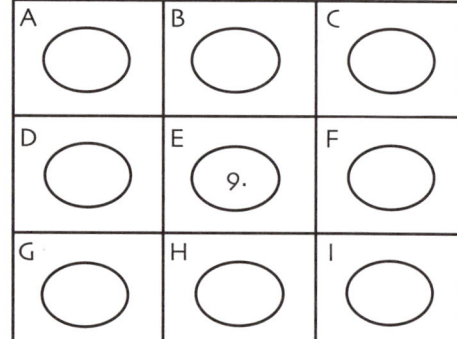

Answers

Woolly Mammoth A9, B8, C1, D6, E7, F5, G4, H3, I2
Rhamphorhynchus A3, B5, C9, D1, E4, F8, G6, H2, I7
Stegosaurus A7, B4, C6, D2, E9, F3, G8, H1, I5

Spot the Differences

Spot 10 differences between the two images.

Answers

27

Make Words

Tyrannosaurus

This "tyrant lizard" was a Cretaceous predator that lived throughout western North America. Its huge head was counter-balanced by its large tail and it could run down prey of all sizes. Its tiny front limbs bore two claws and were unusually powerful at tearing into prey.

How many words can you make from the letters in its name?

Answers

Possible answers include: annoy, ant, array, assort, aunt, aunty, aura, not, nut, ran, rat, roan, roast, rot, runny, runt, runty, rust, sauna, sort, star, stony, story, stray, sunt, tar, ton, toy, tray, turn, unto, urn, yarn, your.

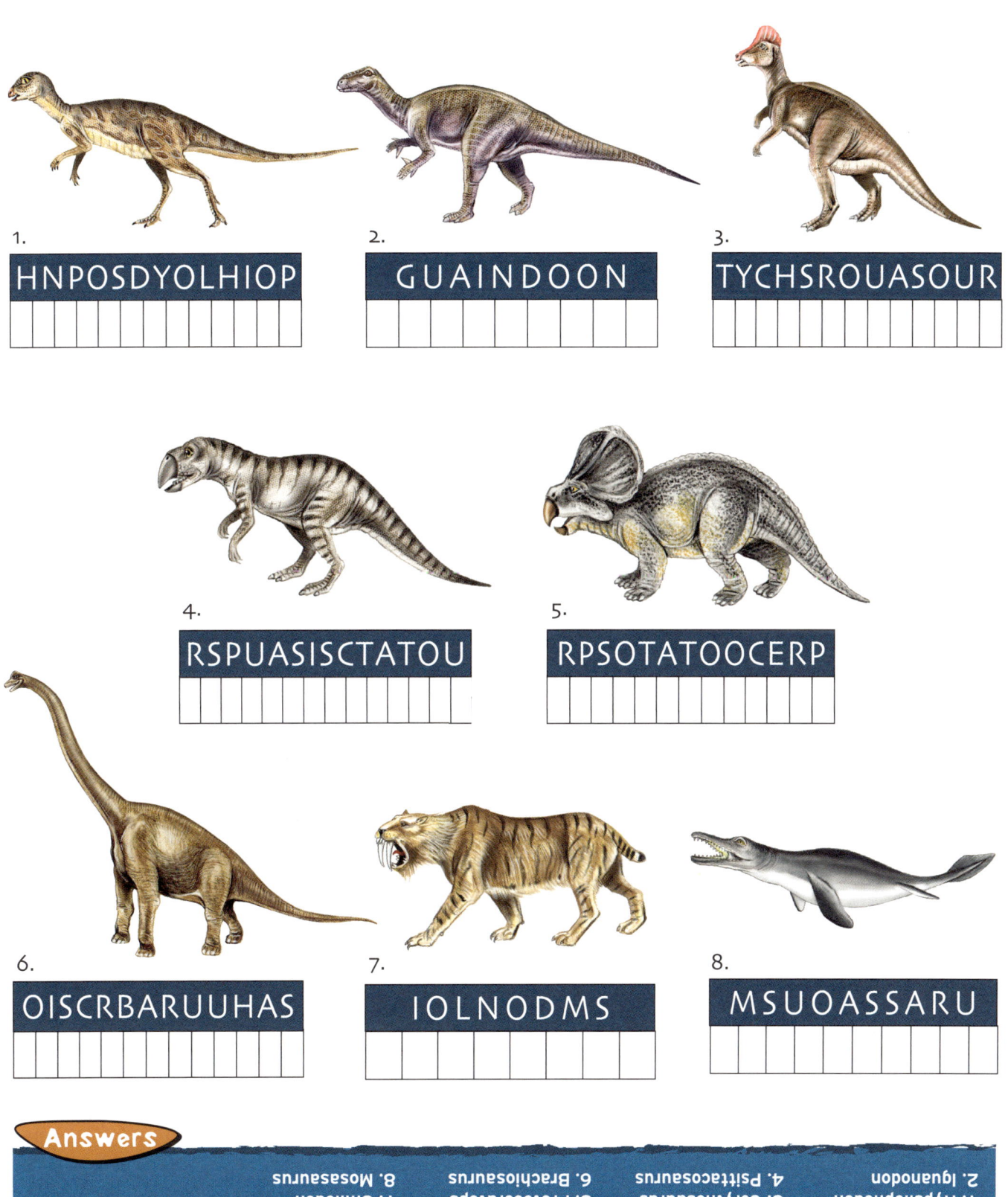

So You're Saying...

Dinosaur names are composed primarily of Latin and Greek words.
For example, raptor = thief; ornith = bird.

Draw a line between the dinosaur and the meaning of its name.

Answers

1. Horned lizard
2. Headless lizard
3. Thick-headed lizard
4. Winged and toothless
5. Ribbon lizard
6. Egg thief
7. Bird imitator
8. Terrible claw

Fold-In

I am a very famous animal that lived 150 million years ago. My name means "ancient-feather-wing" and I was the first fossil to show evidence of feathers. I'm considered a transitional species and a link between reptiles and birds.

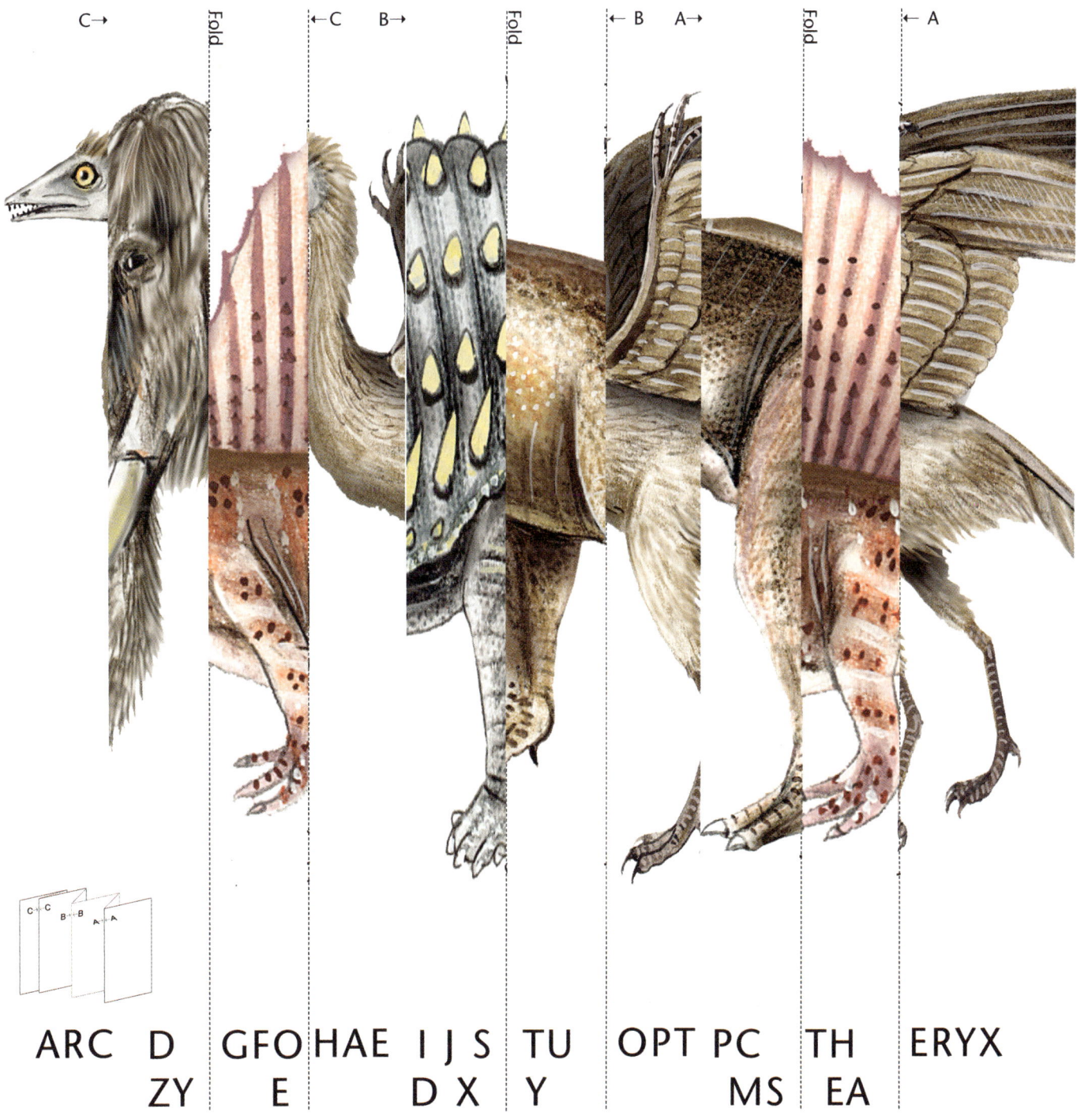

ARC D GFO HAE I J S TU OPT PC TH ERYX
ZY E D X Y MS EA

Word Search

Say it, then find it.

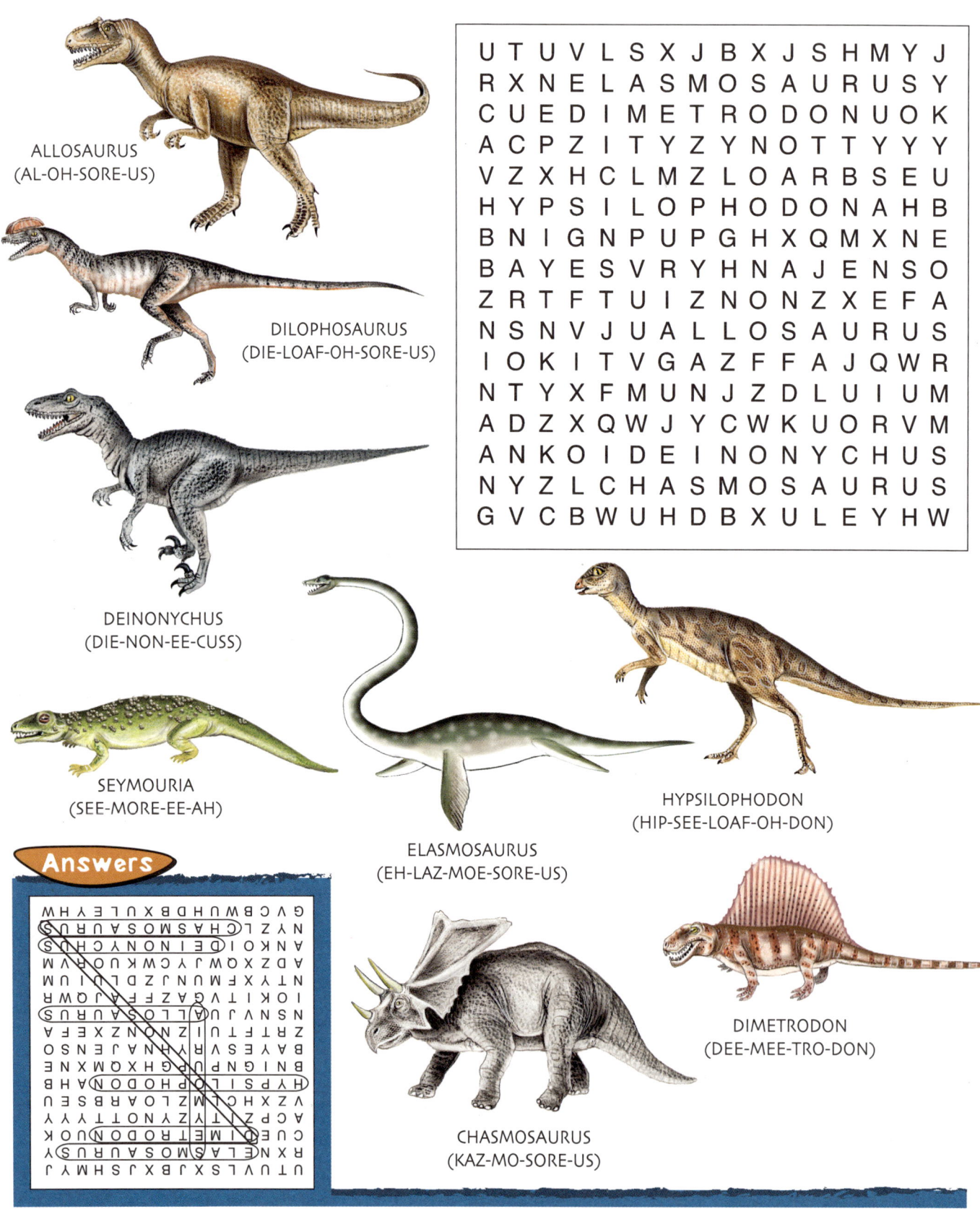

ALLOSAURUS
(AL-OH-SORE-US)

DILOPHOSAURUS
(DIE-LOAF-OH-SORE-US)

DEINONYCHUS
(DIE-NON-EE-CUSS)

SEYMOURIA
(SEE-MORE-EE-AH)

ELASMOSAURUS
(EH-LAZ-MOE-SORE-US)

HYPSILOPHODON
(HIP-SEE-LOAF-OH-DON)

CHASMOSAURUS
(KAZ-MO-SORE-US)

DIMETRODON
(DEE-MEE-TRO-DON)